HANSEL & GRETEL

HANSEL & GRETEL

HOLLY HOBBIE

Little, Brown and Company
New York Boston

*N*ot so long ago, there was a woodcutter who lived with his wife and his two children, Hansel and Gretel, in the shadow of a towering forest. He worked tirelessly, but the times were hard and he could no longer sell enough wood to take care of his family. Each night, they went to bed hungry.

"Listen to me," the wife said. "We cannot feed your children any longer. We must get rid of them." She was the children's stepmother.

"Get rid of them?" the woodcutter shouted. "Never! I love my children."

"Then make four coffins," the wife scolded bitterly. "One for each of us."

With great shame, the woodcutter finally agreed to abandon his children to the forest.

"I'm so afraid," Gretel whispered to Hansel, for she and her brother had overheard their parents discussing their fate.

At the window, Hansel saw bright pebbles glittering on the ground in the moonlight. "Don't worry," he told Gretel. "I will think of something to save us."

In the morning, the woodcutter and his wife took Hansel and Gretel deep into the forest. They built a fire and gave the children meager scraps of bread.

"We must go to work now," their father said. "We will come back before dark to get you."

But the children waited long past dark, and no one came to take them home. "I want to be in my warm bed," Gretel cried.

"We'll soon find our way," her brother told her.

When the moon appeared, a trail of white pebbles gleamed on the ground before them. Hansel had dropped the stones behind him as he and Gretel followed their parents into the woods. The stones led all the way back to the woodcutter's cottage.

The man rejoiced when he saw that his children were safe. The stepmother only pretended to be happy.

"Those two must go," she said to her husband only days later. "And don't argue with me."

This time, as the parents led the children deeper into the forest, Hansel broke up his piece of bread and dropped the crumbs on the path behind him.

Again the woodcutter built a fire to warm them, and he promised to return for them at the end of the day.

As darkness blackened the woods, no one came to take the children home. Soon moonlight illuminated the forest, yet there were no bread crumbs to be found. Birds had eaten every morsel.

Hand in hand, Hansel and Gretel wandered through the woods—hungry, cold, and lost.

Then, on the third morning, they suddenly came upon a cheerful little cottage. The dwelling was made of cake, with a roof of cookies and vanilla icing and windows of sparkling sugar. Hansel and Gretel broke off pieces of sweet chocolate and hungrily ate them.

A woman, bent and withered with age, suddenly stepped into view. "Who dares to nibble at my delicious house?"

When she saw Hansel and Gretel, she grinned from ear to ear.

"Please come in, precious children."

The old woman fed them steaming bowls of soup and creamy pudding. Once they had eaten their fill, she led her two young guests into a cozy room and tucked them into clean, warm beds.

"Can you believe how lucky we are?" Gretel asked drowsily.

"It is hard to believe," said Hansel.

The kind elderly woman was not what she seemed. She was a wicked, red-eyed witch, over one hundred and fifty years old. She liked children; indeed, she liked to eat them for her supper! She had created the irresistible cottage just to entice curious boys and girls into her clutches.

The witch slipped into the bedroom to watch Hansel and Gretel sleep. She sniffed the air. How sweet they smelled. "What a feast awaits me," she whispered.

At dawn, the witch snatched Hansel from his bed and locked him in a wooden cage.

"Now we must fatten him up, girlie," she gloated. And a wild, inhuman cackle escaped her.

"Hansel, you must think of something," Gretel whispered to her brother when she brought him food. "The witch is hungry."

"Maybe you will think of something," Hansel said. "I'm trapped."

Each day, the witch poked through the cage at the boy's ribs and thighs. "Eat more," she cried. "I want my roast to be juicy."

"Gretel, you must do something," Hansel urged. "You must!"

Days passed. At last the witch could wait no longer.

"Fetch wood," she shrieked at Gretel, "while I sharpen my best knife." The next

time Gretel went to the pantry, Hansel pressed his tearful face to the bars of his cage.

"What is going to happen?" he asked. "Is this a nightmare? I must wake up!"

The witch lit the fire to heat the oven.

Soon she ordered Gretel to duck her head inside the dark chamber to see if it was hot enough to bake bread. Gretel knew that it was she—not bread—whom the witch intended to bake. At that instant, the girl experienced a rush of inspiration.

"Duck inside?" she asked. "But how?"

"Silly child!" cried the witch. "You do it like this." She stooped and thrust her head into the mouth of the oven. "Do you see?"

"Yes, I see!" Gretel shouted.

With all her might she shoved against the backside of the witch, and the hideous creature tumbled into the oven. Gretel slammed the heavy door shut and dropped the iron latch in place.

Dreadful shrieks echoed through the still air of the forest. Gretel covered her ears and closed her eyes.

When at last the cries ended, Gretel carefully opened the oven door. There was nothing inside—nothing at all. The witch was gone forever.

Gretel released her brother from his prison, and the two of them hugged and danced and shouted with joy.

Before they fled that awful place, they dared to look through the dusky rooms, where they discovered pearls and precious stones scattered everywhere.

"Can we take them?" asked Gretel.

"Every last one," said Hansel.

They filled their pockets.

At long last, after wandering in the forest for days, they came upon a familiar path. Soon they recognized their father's cottage set among dark hills in dazzling sunlight, and they ran toward it breathlessly.

"Father, we're home!"

Ever since he abandoned his children in the deep woods, the woodcutter had suffered fearful nightmares. His wife, furthermore, had died after eating food that had gone bad. But now unexpected joy overwhelmed him. He held his children close.

Hansel and Gretel were so thrilled to be reunited with their father, they nearly forgot the treasure they'd brought home. They reached into their pockets and displayed handfuls of glowing pearls and precious stones. "Look, Father!"

"Can our cares be over?" the woodcutter asked in awe.

"Yes, yes, yes!" his children sang.

Thereafter, they lived as happily as they knew how.

Artist's Note

In 1947, at age five, I knew how to place the needle of the record player precisely on the groove of the shiny black record to hear the spellbinding voice of the Great Gildersleeve read the transporting tale of Hansel and Gretel, my hands-down favorite story. The pictures that accompanied the story were all in my head, conjured by Gildersleeve's mesmerizing voice. For although my whole family went to the library once a week, returning home with armloads of books, I never saw an illustrated version of Hansel and Gretel there or anywhere else. But then, what could have matched the eerie, magical pictures illuminated by my imagination?

I based my text on *Grimms' Tales for Young and Old*, translated from the German by Ralph Manheim (1977). While I have been faithful to the details of the classic tale, my intention was to let the illustrations speak for themselves, so the text has been shortened substantially from the original. If my book sparks something of that spine tingle I experienced as a child entranced by the Great Gildersleeve, I'll count that as a success.

My paintings are created with transparent watercolor, pen and ink, and gouache on watercolor paper. It was necessary to change my typically cheerful palette to convey the somber setting of Hansel and Gretel. For instance, I found myself using indigo blue for the first time in my life, rather than the brighter and friendlier ultramarine blue. Thank goodness the sun breaks out in the end.

—Holly Hobbie

About This Book

The text was set in Adobe Jenson Pro, and the display type is Baskerville. This book was edited by Andrea Spooner and designed by Tracy Shaw. The production was supervised by Erika Schwartz, and the production editor was Barbara Bakowski.

to Jocelyn